3D WONDERLAND

Part I: *The Evolving Stereogram*

COLUMNS:

The artwork in this book can be viewed in 3D using only the naked eye without any special devices. Those who cannot view these pictures in 3D should consult the instructions on page 18.

Part II: *The Multiplying Stereograms*

↑↑ PARALLEL STYLE / ✕ CROSS-EYED STYLE

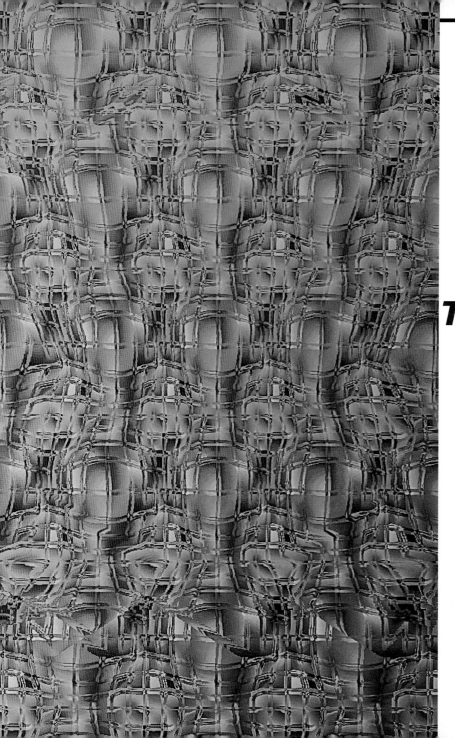

PART I

The Evolving Stereogram

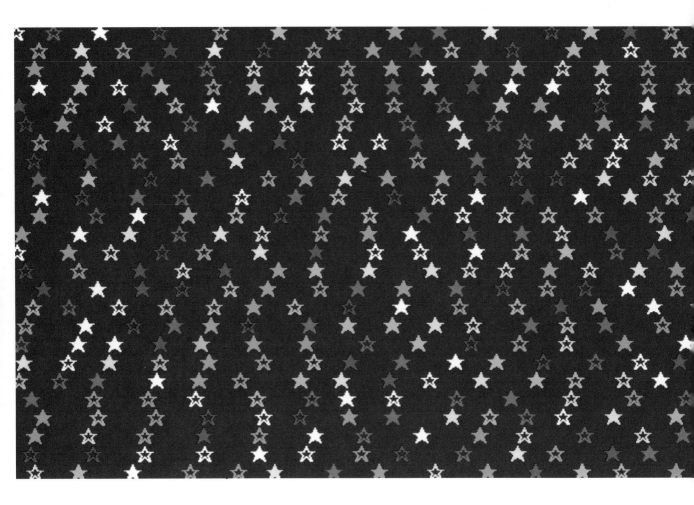

Stars and Stars by O

The sky is filled with stars! This piece of artwork contains two ty
stars in six colors, but when it is viewed in 3D, there are seventy
combinations of colors and shapes. Sixty-six of those will give
variation effect, watch the stars twinkle!

MULTI-FOCUS
STEREOGRAM

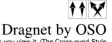

Dragnet by OSO

A net like a mirage that disappears as you view it. (The Cross-eyed Style
tends to be more fun for this picture with its many reference points.)

Compound of Five Octahedra by Shiro Nakaya

(a Japanese translation of Compound of Five Octa

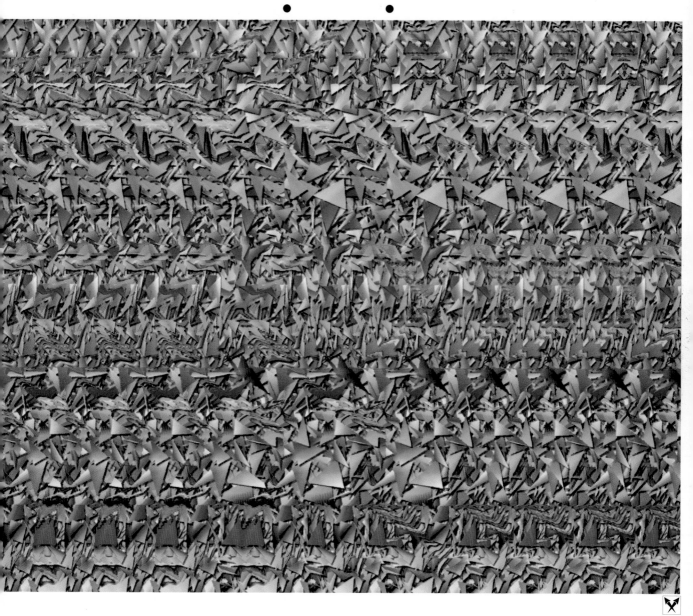

Double Helix by Shiro Nakayama
The double helix of DNA.

RANDOM-TEXTURE STEREOGRAMS

Objects in Dome by OS
A three dimensional graphic where you can see the invis

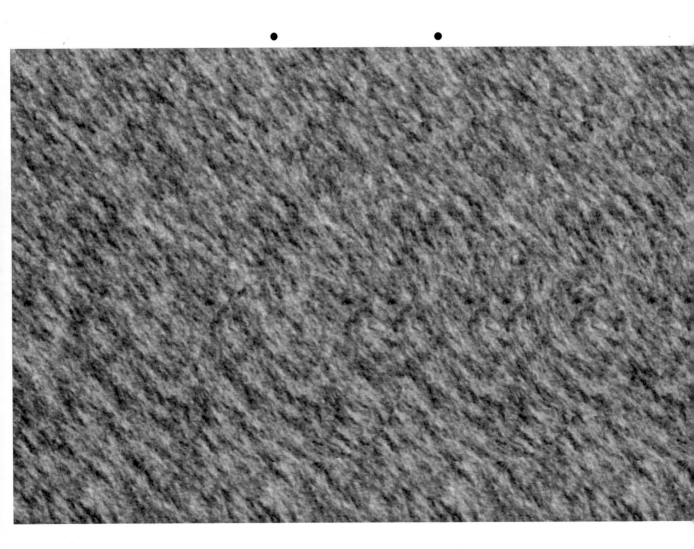

Tunnel Vision by OSO

If you take your time looking at this piece, the depth comes gradually. Before your eyes a vortex appears to draw you in, and you can see through to the other side of the piece. As the surface of the picture gets farther away, it gets more difficult to see the bottom.

  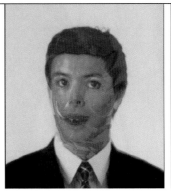 

Morphing is a function of software that blends two different pictures from one to another. These pictures do not actually come out in 3D, but by using 3D viewing techniques, you get quite an interesting effect.

MORPHING

Man to Woman (above) / Beauty to Beast (middle) /
Man to Skeleton (below) by Kan Dava

Using 3D viewing techniques, watch these fascinating changes.

The Gymnastic Ribbon Chorus L
by Kan Da
A line of impressive gymnasts. So, how many gymnasts can you

WALLPAPER STEREOGRAMS

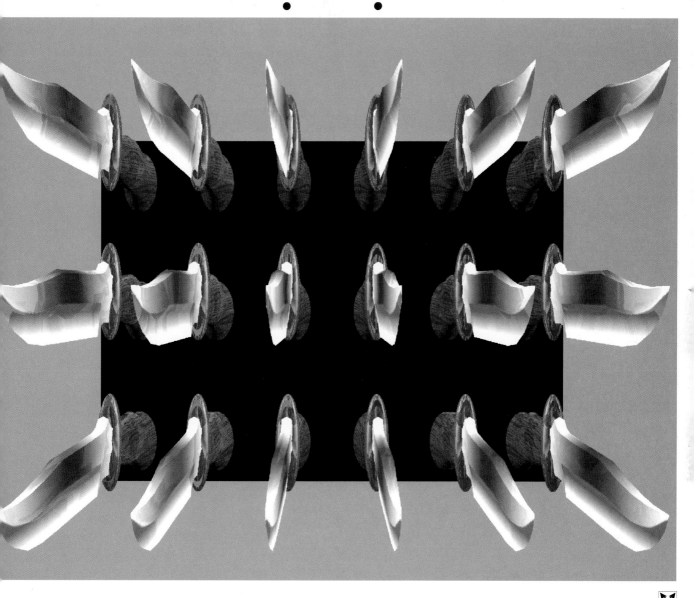

The Ultra Modern Horror Story
by Kan Dava
Get as close to the picture as you dare. As you move the picture away,
the knives get longer.

Escher and the Sky by Kan D[...]

Using original characters and a man-made sky, you get a hint of Es[...]
work. Look through the eyes of ar[...]

COMPUTER GRAPHICS
STEREO PAIRS

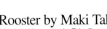
Rooster by Maki Takiya
The colors give a feeling of depth to this stereo pair. This effect was made through a program entitled "P3D." The original work was a glass painting.

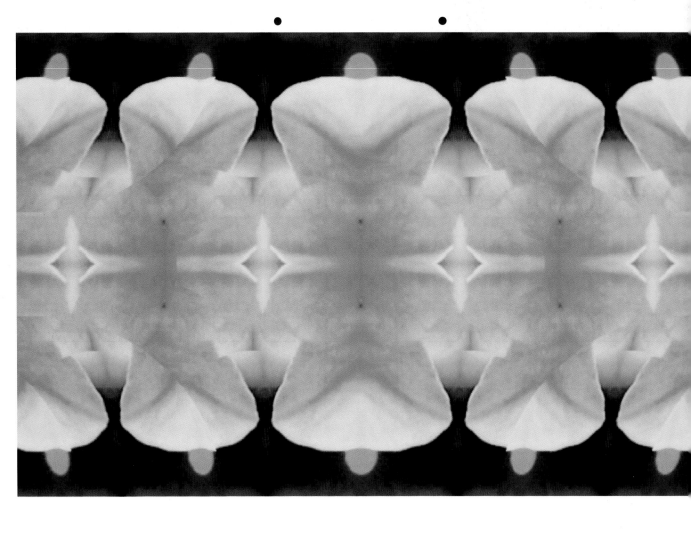

Spherical Haze by O

You can sense a complete sphere in the softness of the
Featuring an extremely delicate texture, the outline of this 3D
seems to vanish in the
(Photo by Fukuzaburo Han

This technique adds the patterns of random
dots with photographs put through special
optics.   These photographs are then put
through a 3D process to make a slightly bent
symmetrical crest pattern.

PHOTOMAPPING
STEREOGRAMS

istance between the cameras for the
Pair (two converging photographs)
ange depending on the distance from
ject being photographed. In this case,
ecial airplane built for Stereo
graphs was used.

STEREO-PHOTOGRAPHS

The Spreading City I by Kozo Ueda
This is a view that cannot be seen with the naked eye. (The high rise district of Shinjuku, Tokyo.)

The Spreading City II by Kozo Ueda
A miniature garden with aerial photography. (Ueno Park, Tokyo.)

Key to Three-Dimensional
Viewing With the Naked Eye

■ After reading through these directions, most people will be able to use the techniques described below to see amazing 3-D pictures.

■ Without learning these techniques, the viewer may not be able to enjoy the exciting new designs of 3-D graphic imaging. In most cases, it takes several minutes of practice and patience, but it will be well worth your time!...

■ The three dimensional images (A.K.A. stereograms) come in two formats: The "Parallel Style" and the "Cross-eyed Style". Each image comes with an icon describing which format it is in.

1 Parallel Style

When a set of human eyes sees an object up close,

they have a tendency to cross. This is due to the way the human brain calculates distance by using two reference points –your eyes. The further away you hold this piece of paper, the more parallel the line of your sight becomes.

■ The Parallel Style imaging was engineered in a way so that when an individual focuses on a distant object while looking at the image up close, your brain is tricked into seeing something three dimensional.

How to view in Parallel Style:

1. First take a deep breath and relax your eyes.

How to view Parallel Style.

Key to Three-Dimensional Viewing With the Naked Eye

2. Pick a distant object and focus your eyes on it.

3. Slowly bring the 3-D picture up into sight but continue focusing on the distant object. The idea is that you pretend to see through the 3-D picture by focusing on something afar. This may take several minutes, if you are trying this for the first time.

4. The two dots on top of the page are there to help you. When you stare at the page out of focus, the two dots should appear as four dots. This is explained by the fact that your eyes are viewing something out of focus and each eye sees double for a total of four.

5. Of the four, two of the inner dots should be over lapped. Now concentrate on these two inner dots and try to bring them together as one.

6. Once the two dots blend into one, focus on it. The image should now be three-dimensional!

■ In the Parallel Style, the image intended for the right eye is on the right side, and the image intended for the left eye is printed on the left side of the art.
■ When the lines of vision for the right and left eyes point straight ahead, the picture appears 3-dimensional. Due to this, one cannot separate the information in the two images beyond a certain distance. That distance is usually about 2 3/4" or 7 cm.

Reference Picture 1

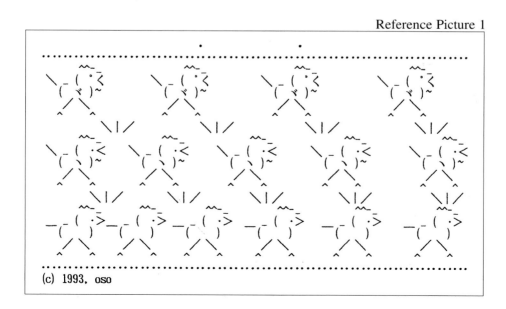

(c) 1993, oso

II Cross-eyed Style:

■ The Cross-eyed Style is the opposite of the Parallel Style. Initially, the viewer must begin by focusing on a point closer than the actual image to get the eyes crossed. In this approach, you focus on an image on the right with the left eye and on an image on the left with the right eye.

■ Where the Parallel Style uses parallel eye positions when looking at something far away, the Cross-eyed Style uses cross-eyed positions when looking at something very close. Your line of sight must be as if looking at something close when your focus is on something further away.

1. Bring your pointing finger up close to your eyes and stare at it to get cross-eyed. This is done so that your eyes can focus on a point closer than the image.

2. Continue focusing on your finger and look at the picture. As with the Parallel Style, you should be able to see four dots.

3. Move your finger back and forth until the two inner dots blend into one. (This should be a lot easier to do than the Parallel Style.)

4. Of the three images, concentrate and focus on the center image. The important point to remember is to keep your eyes crossed but keeping focused far at the same time.

How to view Cross -eyed Style.

5. As with the previous style this takes time and patience but with a few minutes of practice, you should be able to see the wonderful effects of 3-D imaging!

■ With the Cross-eyed Style, the stereo images will appear smaller than when the pictures are viewed normally. Another feature is that there is more freedom in the size of the artwork.

■ The information (image) on the right side is viewed with the left eye, and the information on the left side is viewed with the right eye, so there is more freedom in how far apart the information can be separated. A large poster can still be seen if you stand back a little ways from the wall.

Reference Picture 2

```
      PICSヲ飲ミ込ムム時間獣            PICSヲ飲ミ込ムム時間獣
 ---------------------------    ---------------------------
  << TIME  ZOOooooooooo....NnnE >>    <<TIME  ZOOooooo...NnnE>>


PICS)                    o         (PICS)                  o
 >------ >               ~~~         >------  >            ~~~
   >====  (                          >====  (
      >=====  (                         >=====  (
        >              x                  >             x
```

(c) 1992, oso

Reference Picture 3

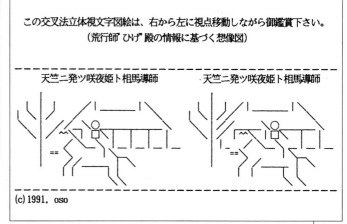

この交叉法立体視文字図絵は、右から左に視点移動しながら御鑑賞下さい。
（荒行師 ひげ 殿の情報に基づく想像図）

天竺ニ発ツ咲夜姫ト相馬導師　　　天竺ニ発ツ咲夜姫ト相馬導師

(c) 1991, oso

•The reference pictures introduced here were images introduced at the Nifty Serve Forum.

3D and Working the Eyes

An interview with Dr. Nobue Kubota, Professor of Optometry at Teikyo University. (Tokyo, Japan)

•*Do you ever use 3D illustrations in Optometry?*

■ **Kubota** - We use machines that test to see if both the eyes are working at the same level. One method uses polarized light, and in the second method one picture is in red and one in green (random dot style). In this method the subject wears red and green glasses to separate the colors for each eye. In either case, the image will be different for the left eye than the image for the right eye. In some cases the difference will be very small; where the differences are largest, the subject will see the greatest 3D effect. The illustrations we use for examinations are usually man-made.

•*So when you look at it normally, it will look 3D.*

■ **Kubota** - Exactly. There is no strain in the natural process of "adjustment" (focus) and "convergence" (crossing of the lines of sight). Because there is a balance between adjustment and convergence, the subject should be able to see a dramatic 3D image unless the balance is off.

•*In naked eye 3D viewing, we don't use any corrective devices in viewing the image in 3D. Would you say that this is a somewhat unnatural condition?*

■ **Kubota** - When you view the image you separate your adjustment and convergence. In the Cross-eyed method, the image exceeds the convergence. For example, if the image is held thirty centimeters from the eyes, your eyes converge at a point closer. A thirty centimeter target might converge at a ten centimeter point. Since convergence and adjustment are normally balanced, your eyes would normally adjust to (focus on) a point ten centimeters from your eyes. But your eyes adjust to a point thirty centimeters away, so the balance is broken. In the Parallel Style method, the eyes take a divergent path. Normally humans are much more comfortable with a convergent path, so I believe that the Parallel Style method is the more difficult method.

•*The Cross-eyed method is easier?*

■ **Kubota** - Yes. Normally one cannot separate the eyes voluntarily. Crossing your eyes, you can voluntarily converge some 20 to 40 degrees. But normally you cannot separate them more than two or three degrees.

•*I was able to use the Parallel Style before the Cross-eyed Style.*

■ **Kubota** - I suppose those who are slightly walleyed might have an easier time with the Parallel Style. Walleyed means that when one eye is hidden, the other will naturally move to the side. Perhaps near sighted people who have trouble focusing on far off objects anyway, might find the Parallel Style easier.

•*There seem to be many people who are not able to view naked eye 3D. Are there any medical reasons why this might be?*

■ **Kubota** - First of all, people with strabismus. Strabismus is a condition where the position of one eye is not connected with the position of the other. Even when seeing with both eyes, they don't form a composite image, and cannot see in 3D. Then there are those whose eye strength is different. If one has an eye strength of less than 0.1, I guess they would not be able to view this process.

•*When you view a naked eye 3D image, might there be problems with your eyes?*

■ **Kubota** - When you stare at anything for a long time, you may get eye strain. One thinks nothing of whether their eyes are getting better or worse when looking at the normal world. As far as I know, there is no connection with your eye strength and viewing. However, if you destroy the balance of adjustment and convergence, you invite an imbalance of the autonomous nerves.

■ This type of viewing by those with autonomic ataxia, and those with the beginnings of farsightedness caused by old age could cause an instability of the autonomic nerves and should avoid attempting naked eyed 3D viewing. When one looks at these images for a long time, it may cause dizziness or nausea. People with ametropia such as hypermetropia or astigmatism may tire more easily when viewing these images.

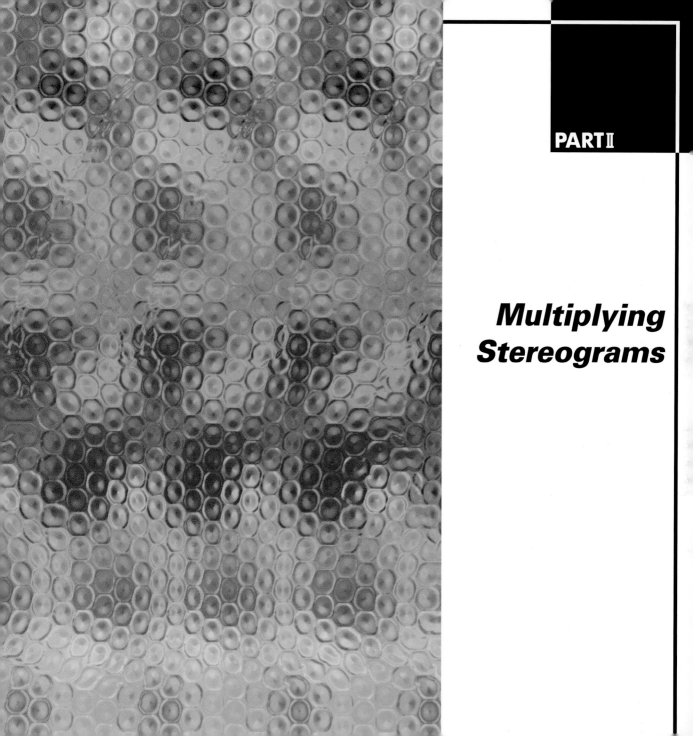

PART II

Multiplying
Stereograms

ANIMALS

The Teddy Bear by Shiro Nakayama
The face of a bear.

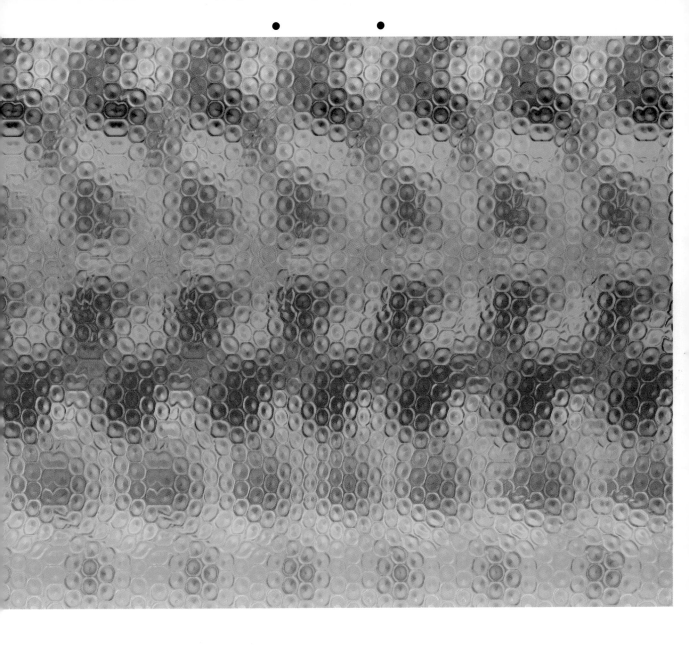

Rabbit by Shiro Nakayama
face of a rabbit.

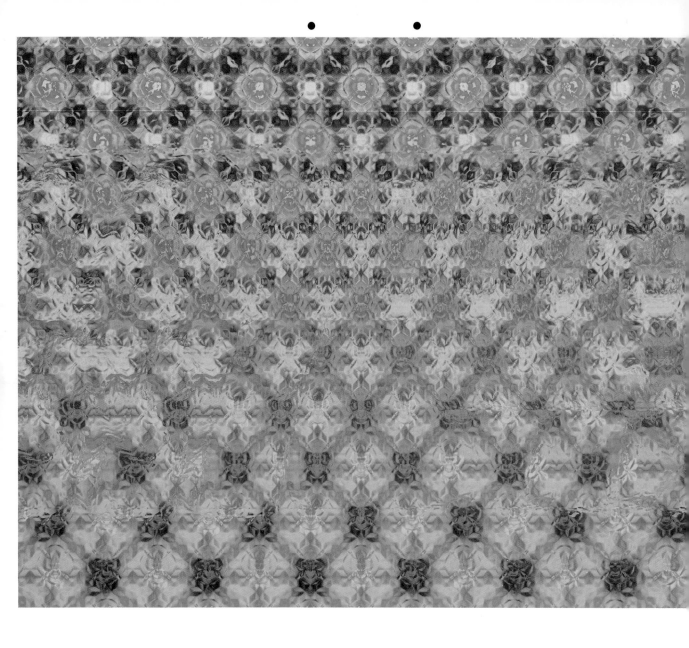

The Elephant by Shiro Nakayama
An entire elephant facing sideways.

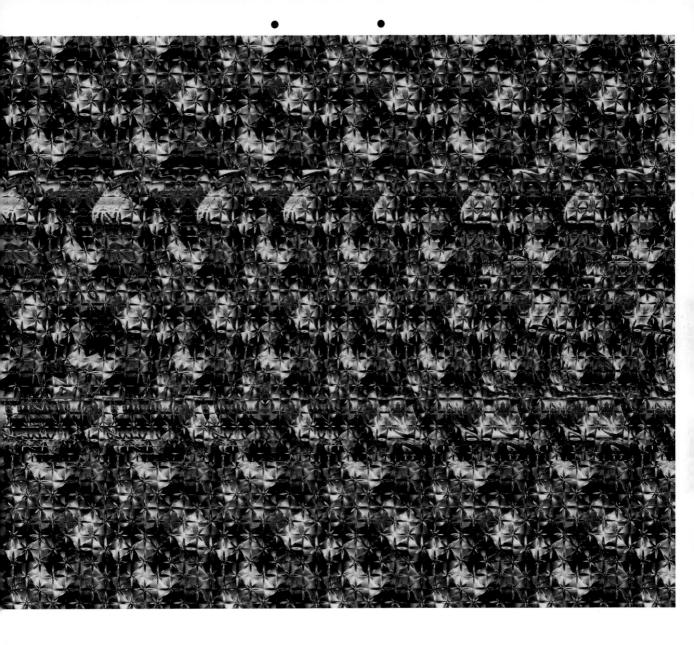

Stegosaur by Shiro Nakayama
ntire stegosaurs.

GEOMETRIC 3D

Cylindrical Cave by OSO
Massive columns, cold water and rocks of a
mountain stream.

Hyperbolic Pillars by OSO
the hyperbolic mounds as they swirl past
rock walls.   (Photo by Fukuzaburo Hamada)

THE FOUR SEASONS

Spring by Kengo Tsukasaki
See the spring sky behind the falling cherry blossoms.

Summer by Kengo Tsukas
A summer shower as seen from ab

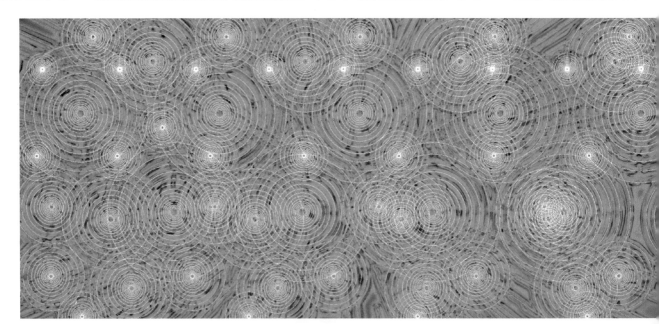

l by Kengo Tsukasaki
untains of colored leaves falling silently
m the trees to the Earth.

Winter by Kengo Tsukasaki
Catch it in your hand and it disappears. Snow
falling like crystal pixies.

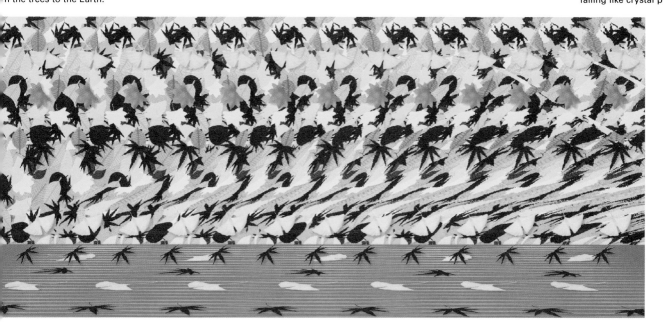

Winter by Kengo Tsukasaki
Catch it in your hand and it disappears. Snow
falling like crystal pixies.

THE ROOM OF COCO THE CAT

My Amusing Home & Summer by Maki Takiya
Viewed in 3D the room looks bigger. Pay attention to
the man on the television.

gy Liggy Lo by Maki Takiya
cat in the nation of toys.

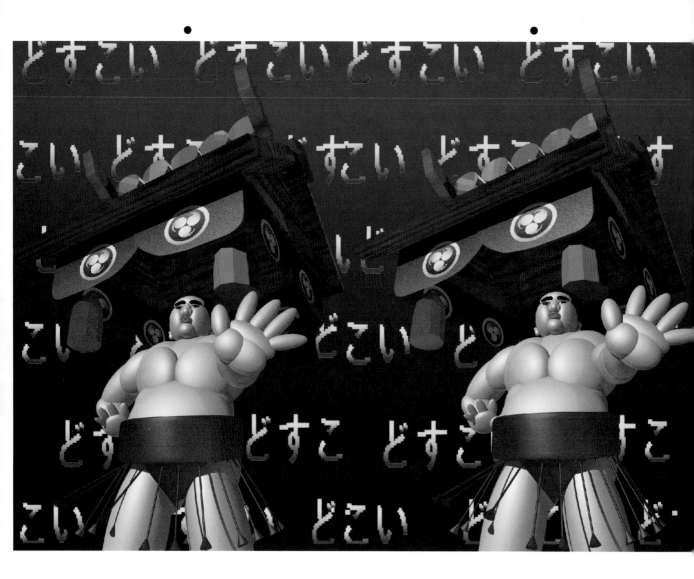

SUMO WRESTLER

Dosukoi by Ma-mi Dava
A 3DCG (computer graphic) of a wrestler.
When viewed, the space comes alive.

e Dangerous Match: Who Won? by Ma-mi Dava
o won? View it in 3D and find out. (The wrestler who
ches the ground first loses.)

3D MANDALA

Golden Banquet by Ma-mi Dava
Objects reflected in the golden mirror. This
sight cannot be seen except in 3D.

The NIFTY-Serve 3D Discussion Group

■ With the recent 3D boom, quite a few different fields have been joined. One of these fields is the NIFTY-Serve personal computer network.

■ When you have a telephone connecting an input/output device, called a modem, connected to your personal computer, you can access these networks. On a network, you can acquire the latest information faster than reading publications, listening to the radio, or watching television. You can access databases, or access local or regional business communication networks. It has been called the information age media. NIFTY-Serve is Japan's foremost personal computer network encompassing more than five hundred thousand users. On the "forums," themed user groups, there are activities encompassing all kinds of subjects and interests. Several years ago, naked eye 3D viewing became a topic of interest on many of these forums. Many stereograms were published, and a lively exchange of information ensued. We would like to introduce a few representative forums (where messages are written and read forming a discussion) and some of the activities on them:

■ "Psychology Forum (FPSY) : Parapsychology" This is a forum for discussing the many aspects of psychology. In April of 1991, the discussion of naked eye 3D spilled over from FBEAT, and was the foundation for several clues that allowed software in 3D computer graphics to be created. Psychology is very concerned with the sense of sight and the research has spawned not only the random dot style, but many other styles of 3D viewing. People interested in the mechanisms involved in 3D should like this forum.

■ "PICS Forum (FPICS): Salon Bermuda, Mysterious 3D, The 3D Image Preparation Forum". This is a forum for computer graphic professionals and artists to share and exchange pictures in the GIF format. (The most widely used format in the world for picture information.) In 1991, a boom occurred in the distribution of large sized Cross-eyed Style 3D pictures. The boom ended with a library of pictures, images, and simple animations in 3D. Recently, there has been quite a bit of discussion on hard 3D imaging such as holograms or lenticulars, and the 3D Image Preparation Forum is established for that.

■ "QLD Laboratories (FQLD2): 3D research lab"
This is the support forum for Japan's foremost image maker, the QLD company. They were at the center of the industry when the first 3D viewers came out. Recently they've added the Parallel Style naked eye 3D artwork to their line. One may obtain many of their computer graphics and hand paintings over the computer using this forum.

■ "Movie Forum (FMOVIE): Brain Resort Development Lab"
More than a discussion on the techniques of 3D, the Brain Resort Development Lab (Stereo Fan Discussion Group) was formed to discuss the development of 3D. And the group is dedicated to enjoying and spreading a relaxed mental attitude. It's a unique group that has followed the "stereomania" path to mental health and concentration for a very long time. The discussion is a charming flow-of-consciousness conversation that could go anywhere.

■ "The Personal Computer System Japanese Environment Forum (FJAMES): Design Miso Warehouse"
Japanese language environment for personal computer systems is not a topic that would relate much to 3D, but many interesting developments have come out of this forum. Graphic professionals and artists, especially those working on techniques with the Macintosh® computer system, have come up with many famous stereogram wallpapers and published them on this forum.

■ Other forums such as FBEAT, FART, and FQUIZ also have discussions on 3D.
Contact NIFTY-Serve at: 03-5471-5800. NIFTY Serve is based in Japan. All services related to this network are in Japanese.

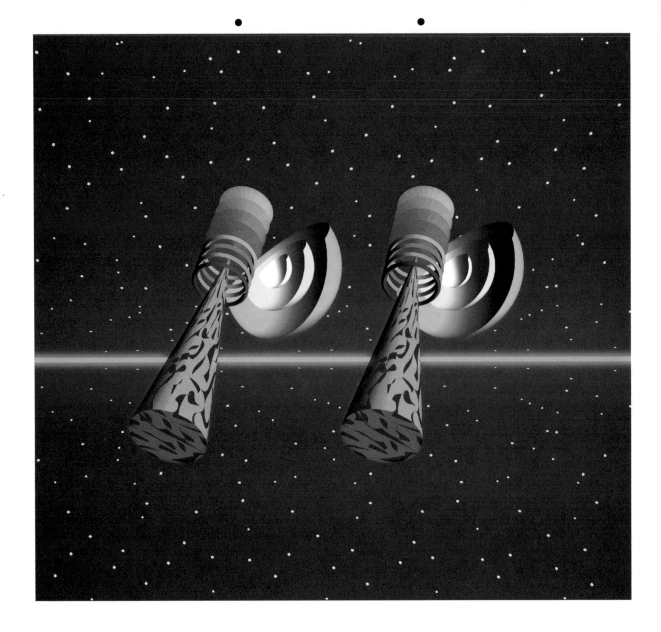

FLYING LETTERS

P by Senei Karino
Letters flying through space.

y Senei Karino
rs written in a fantasy space.

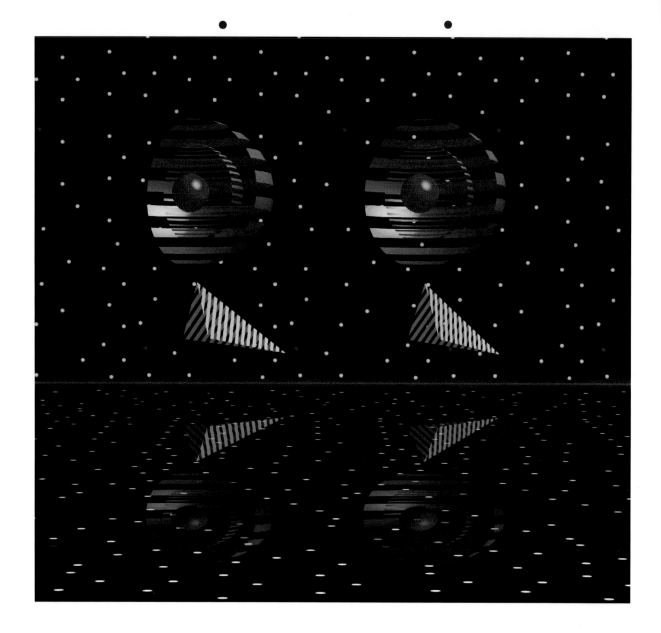

R by Senei Karino
A reflection different from water or a mirror.

Dancing Letter by Ma-mi Dava
This one can be appreciated as a picture on its own,
but as you use 3D, the objects come out at you.

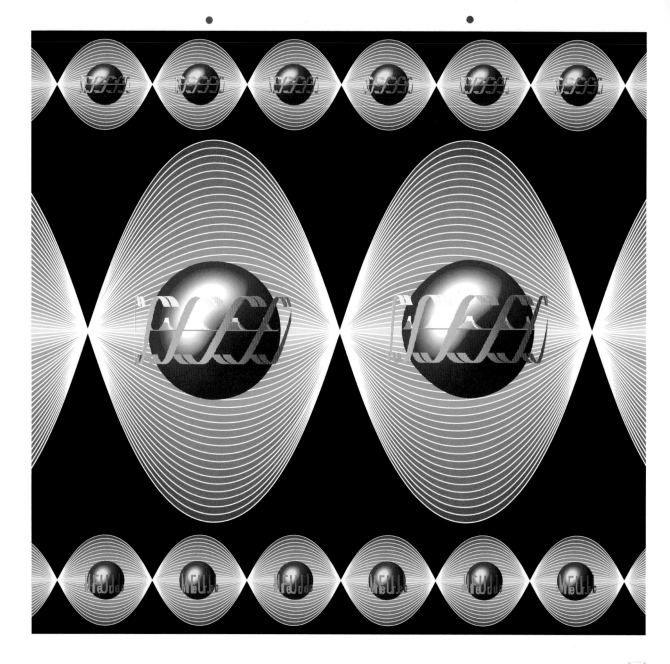

WAVE

sMtFeUrJeIo by Kurima Numata
Mt. Fuji inside the wave, a very Japanese style graphic.

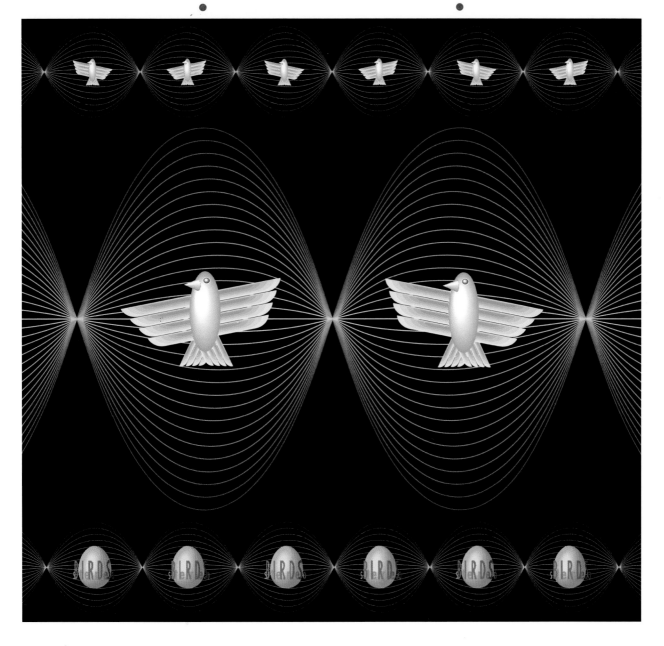

eRrDeSo by Kurima Numata
en viewed in 3D, the wings seem to flap. Strange
. . .

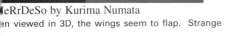

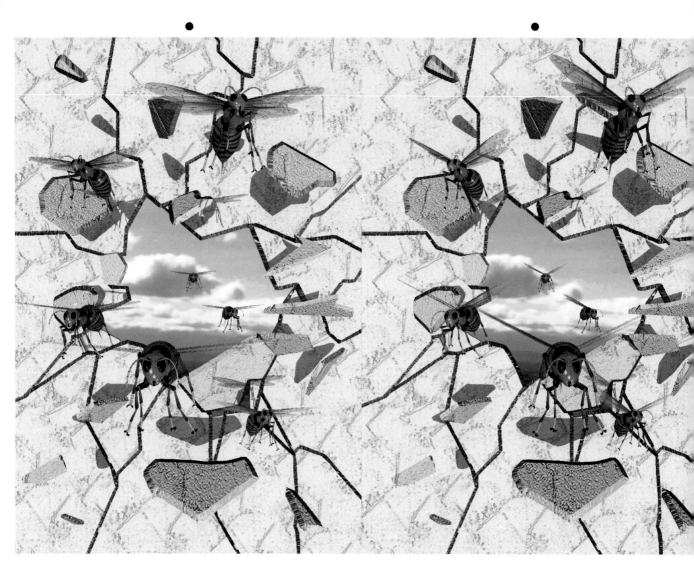

CLASS B ANGELS

Bee Raid by Kan Dava
You can almost hear the buzzing of the wings. What's
that itchy, painful feeling?

...ed or Eaten? by Kan Dava
...angel is being chased by the frightening dinosaur.
...an it escape from the gaping jaws?

44-45

QUICK, EASY AND PAINLESS

To You Who Have Your Own Anxieties by Eiichi Misaka
A fish (Mambo) swims in a half sphere of water, as the chains come to bind him.

You Who Chastise Yourself for a Guilty Conscience by Eiichi Misaka
...uirrel who has gathered together red hearts caught amid a thicket of painful thorns.

To You Who Love Red Flowers by Eiichi Misaka
A raw computer graphic. Every other rose makes a stereo pair.

COMPUTER GRAPHIC GLASS PICTURES

Stairs by Maki Takiya

Colors float on the surface of these processed stereograms. You get a completely different sense of depth when viewed in 3D.

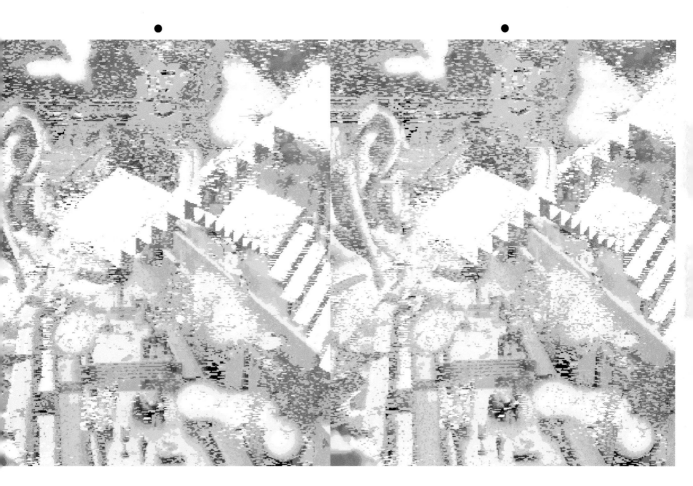

Ball by Maki Takiya

When the third dimension is expressed in the light and dark, but not in the ball, it seems a bit strange.

nd by Maki Takiya

s is a photograph that was converted to a stereogram by the
D" program. The composition is so chaotic, it seems less like
D picture and more like twin view artwork.

THE SKY AND
THE EARTH

The Sky and the Earth I by Kozo Ueda
A vapor spirit that is rising to escape from the clouds.

The Sky and the Earth II by Kozo Ueda
Strange clouds in the wind and the land spreading below.

Sky and the Earth III by Kozo Ueda
contrast between the desert and the sea.

Sky and the Earth IV by Kozo Ueda
Grand Canyon.

Sky and the Earth V by Kozo Ueda
underside of a line of clouds.

Light and Darkness I by Kozo Ueda
The lights of a fantasy market stall. (Hong Kong)

Light and Darkness II by Kozo Ueda
The center of the sparkler draws a spiral picture as it turns.

↑↑

ow Scenes I by Kozo Ueda
e snow brings out the shape of each building.

ow Scenes II by Kozo Ueda
powdered face of an 1800's home.

ow Scenes III by Kozo Ueda
nely world in the snow.

Artist -- Pages

In cooperation with Seizan-sha
Cover Design - Ten Graephis (Masahiko Komuro)

3D WONDERLAND

American Edition published in 1993 by TOKUMA SHOTEN PUBLISHING CO., LTD., 1150 SKYLINE TOWER, 10900 NE 4TH, BELLEVUE, WA 98004.
Originally published in Japan by TOKUMA SHOTEN PUBLISHING CO., LTD., Tokyo in 1993, Publisher/Yasuyoshi Tokuma, Producer/Koichi Chikaraishi. ©1993 TOKUMA SHOTEN Printed and bound in Japan.

Publisher	Tsutomu Otsuka
Producer	Yoshio Tsuboike
Translation	WIlliam Flanagan
Editing	Eugene H. Saburi
Director of Marketing	Dennis Edlund

ISBN4-19-086977-5